OUR FATHER
INSPIRATION OF
G✝D

Evalena C. Robinson
Illustrated by Kierrah Williams

Library of Congress Control Number: 2022917012
ISBN-13:   Paperback: 978-1-64749-839-9
                Hardcover   978-1-64749-841-2
                ePub: 978-1-64749-840-5

Printed in the United States of America

GoToPublish LLC
1-888-337-1724
www.gotopublish.com
info@gotopublish.com

OUR FATHER
INSPIRATION OF
G✝D

Evalena C. Robinson
Illustrated by Kierrah Williams

One spring day as little Billy sat swinging from his tree swing in his grandma's back yard; he began to wonder about the words he heard his mama saying each night before she turns out the lights.

As he sat swinging, he began to slow down and finally came to a sudden stop. He had a strange look on his face and suddenly he began to speak in a soft and tender voice. "Our Father, why are you in heaven and not here with me?" A voice so gentle and sweet replied, "Billy my child, I am in heaven to prepare a place for you, and someday I will come back to get you and bring you here to live with me forever." Then it became very quiet.

Billy spoke softly once again saying, "Our Father, what does hallowed be thy name mean?" The sweet gentle voice replied once again. "Billy, my child, it means to be set apart as Holy. To honor and respect who I AM, the Father of your Spirit. Some of my people have not yet realized I AM the Father of their Spirit and I AM with them always. I promised in My Holy Word never to leave them or forsake them."

Billy then asked, "Our Father, when will your kingdom come?" "Billy my child" the voice said, "My Kingdom has come through My son Jesus Christ, when you received him in your heart. You can also see the kingdom come when others let Christ into their lives and change their lives to be more like him." Billy thought about that for a moment.

Then Billy said "Our Father, why isn't your will being done on earth as it is in heaven?" It was silent for a minute, and then the sweet soft voice said, "My child, in heaven the angels praise me. They worship me all the day long. They honor me. They respect me for who I AM. They appreciate me. They value me and, most of all, they love and obey my commands. On earth, my people have no respect for those whom they are with all of the time, so they don't respect who I AM."

"They only worship me on Sunday, and call me only if they are in need. They don't praise me enough for all that I do, and don't do as I ask of them in my word. They have brought shame instead of glory unto my name."

Little Billy said immediately, "Our Father, then why do you give us your daily bread?" Yet again the soft sweet voice replied, "My child, I feed you the bread of life daily, which is my word, and if you eat of it you will grow strong. Then you will be able to withstand the trials and temptations of this world." Little Billy paused a few seconds to collect his thoughts.

"Our Father, why do you forgive us our debts?" Billy asked. Immediately that soft sweet voice replied, "Billy my child, many years ago, I came to earth to live with my people. They rejected me and nailed me to a cross and there I paid a debt I did not owe. Yet I loved them so much, I said to myself, 'These are my people. I will forgive them for they know not what they have done.' To show my love towards them, I will pay their debts in full upon the cross."

Little Billy was so excited, he began to twist around in his swing; then he asked, "Our Father, is this why you ask us to forgive our debtors?" The soft sweet voice said, "Yes my child, it is very important that you forgive others of their wrongs, just as I have forgiven those who did me wrong. This will show my love for you, and remember always, if you do as I did and follow after me, you will live in heaven with me forever."

As little Billy listened to the soft sweet voice, he became very quiet. After the voice had finished and was quiet once again, little Billy started to swing back and forth. As he swung, he began to talk. "Our Father, why did you not lead us into temptation?" He waited for a moment to listen for the sweet soft voice, but he heard nothing.

Then he said to himself, that soft sweet voice must have gotten tired of answering all those questions. Suddenly he heard something and said, "Is that you little voice?" The soft sweet voice explained "Remember my child I'm always near and to answer your question; I lead you away from temptation, it can cause you to stumble and fall. It is a very powerful tool that the devil uses to lead my people away from me. So I lead you by my word away from temptation and toward righteousness. If you will obey my commandments and follow my laws, I will lead you in the path of righteousness for my name sake. Then I will know you are always with me."

Little Billy wanted to hear more so he asked, "Our Father, how can you deliver us from evil?" The soft sweet voice said, "My child, I have sent to you a part of myself called the Holy Spirit to live inside your heart. He leads you in the right way, so that no evil will be able to overtake your mind, your body nor your soul." By this time, little Billy was too excited to swing anymore. So he got off the swing and sat beside the large oak tree. "Our Father, where is your kingdom?" Billy asked.

The soft sweet voice replied, "Billy, My kingdom is in heaven, where I live and watch you play every day and sleep each night. It's high above the clouds, so as I sit on my throne I can look beneath the clouds and see everything happening in the world, both good and bad. Billy, do you remember when I told you that My kingdom had come through My son Jesus? Well, when you received him into your heart, then My kingdom also came in you."

Billy said, "I have enjoyed talking and listening to you. Do you have time to answer some more of my questions?" Without a reply Billy said, "Our Father, who has the power?" The soft sweet voice replied "Billy my child, all power belongs to me, but because I love my people so much, I have given each one a measure of it through faith, so they will be able to live in peace here on earth. You must have some power to rule over the darkness of the present world."

Little Billy didn't waste any time before asking, "What is the glory?" "Billy," the soft sweet voice explained, "The glory is a form of love shown to someone by praising them for doing well or being good and kind. Glory shows great honor to those who do well. When my people obey my commandments and live by my word, it brings glory and honor to me, letting me know they love me. Therefore, my glory shines in their lives for the entire world to see."

Little Billy put his right hand under his small chin, and asked, "Was it forever?" The soft sweet voice explained to Billy, "Forever is always, it is at all times. Just as I promised, I will be with you at all times. I will never leave you." Wasting no time, little Billy asked, "Our Father, is A-men your son?" The soft sweet voice grew a bit louder saying, "Billy my child, A-men is not a person; but it also belongs to me! I created A-men to say to my people: it may be so, to express to them agreement or approval, certainty, or its okay with me and to bring it to an end."

Once again little Billy grew very quiet. For about two minutes, he said nothing at all. Finally he said, "Our Father, I want to thank you for taking the time out of your busy schedule to spend time with me and answer all of my questions. I promise always to honor, respect, and revere your name and your word. I promise to forgive other people, love everyone, give you glory, stay away from temptation, call and not hollow out your name, eat your bread daily, use your power to stay away from evil, and love you forever. Thank you Father, for helping me to know that Your Kingdom has come into my heart and one day I will come to the place you have prepared for me in heaven. I promise to pray every day like mama."

Our Father, which art in heaven, Hallowed be thy name. Thy kingdom come. Thy will be done in earth, as it is in heaven. Give us this day our daily bread. And forgive us our debts, as we forgive our debtors. And lead us not into temptation, but deliver us from evil: For thine is the kingdom, the power, and the glory forever. A-men

THE END

Special Acknowledgements to:
Two Great Men and Woman of God
Reverend Sidney and Barbara Payton
Warren P. Culbertson III
And
My Beloved Husband
Leon (Robbie) Robinson

About the Author

EVALENA C. ROBINSON has passionately raised four children and enthusiastically surrounded herself with her grandchildren and godchildren often. She is also known as "Sweet E" to a number of other children whom she has taught, became an adoptive parent to, loved or has come in contact with. Her main desire is to see children come to the knowledge of Christ at an early age.

In 1979, she earned a Bachelor of Science degree in Children Development from the University of South Carolina. Since then she has used this degree in multitude of ways. She has worked as a teacher's assistant, private care provider for children, as a children's church coordinator, and so much more.

Printed in the USA
CPSIA information can be obtained
at www.ICGtesting.com
LVHW071926060923
757402LV00021B/831